A Rumbly Tumbly Glittery Gritty Place

A Rumbly Tumbly Glittery Gritty Place

MARY LYN RAY

ILLUSTRATED BY

DOUGLAS FLORIAN

HARCOURT BRACE & COMPANY

SAN DIEGO   NEW YORK   LONDON

Library of Congress Cataloging-in-Publication Data
Ray, Mary Lyn.
A rumbly tumbly glittery gritty place/Mary Lyn Ray;
illustrated by Douglas Florian.
p.   cm.
Summary: A child describes all the wonderful things there are
to enjoy in the gravel pit across the road.
ISBN 0-15-292861-8
[1. Rocks — Fiction.] I. Florian, Douglas, ill. II. Title.
PZ7.R210154Ru   1993
[E] — dc20   92-20084

Printed in Singapore
First edition
A B C D E

For Sylvia and Paul, and Sam
— M. L. R.

For Brigitte Lallouz
— D. F.

Across the road there is a gravel pit.

It is a place to watch machines in:

loaders, shovels, dozers.

Some grown-ups think it's ugly.

More than I have pockets for.

Gray rocks, brown rocks, pink rocks,

shiny rocks.

It is a beach without an ocean.

It is mountains I can climb.

of deer and bear, who come at night.

whose milk I drink.

But now it is still

scrapes and piles

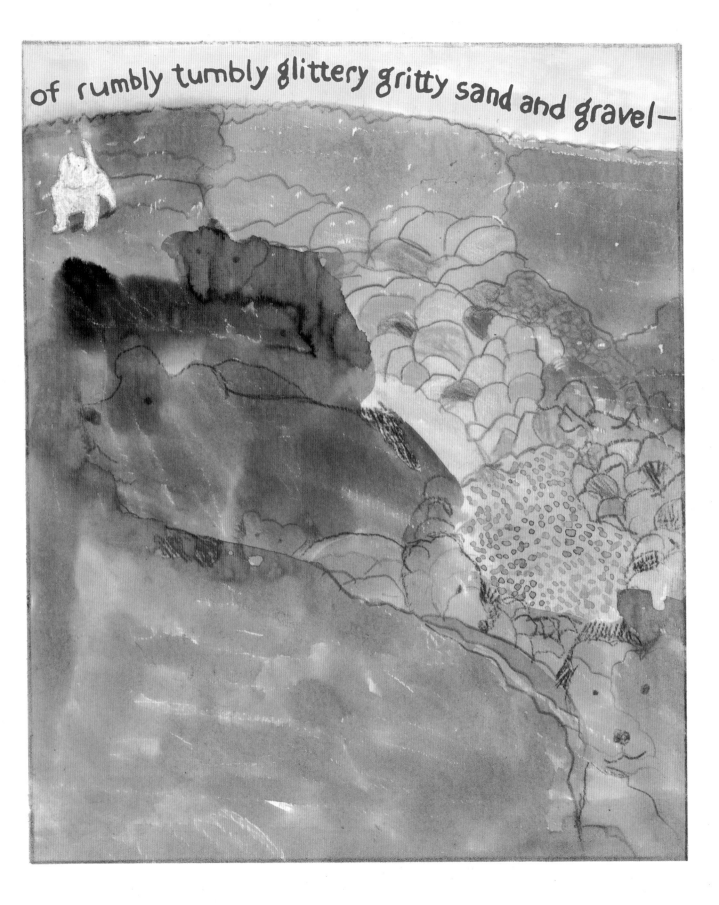

of rumbly tumbly glittery gritty sand and gravel—

I love.

The illustrations in this book were done
in pen-and-ink and watercolor on vellum paper.
The display type was set in Simoncini Garamond.
The text type was hand-lettered by the illustrator.
Color separations by Bright Arts, Ltd., Singapore
Printed and bound by Tien Wah Press, Singapore
Production supervision by Warren Wallerstein and Ginger Boyer
Designed by Lisa Peters